My
Little House
Birthday Book

My Little House Birthday Book

ADAPTED FROM THE LITTLE HOUSE BOOKS

by Laura Ingalls Wilder

Illustrated by Deborah Maze

■ HarperFestival®

A Division of HarperCollinsPublishers

Birth Symbols

MONTH	BIRTH FLOWER	BIRTHSTONE
January	Carnation	Garnet
February	Violet	Amethyst
March	Jonquil	Aquamarine
April	Sweet pea	Diamond
May	Lily of the valley	Emerald
June	Rose	Pearl
July	Larkspur	Ruby
August	Gladiolus	Sardonyx
September	Aster	Sapphire
October	Marigold	Opal
November	Chrysanthemum	Topaz
December	Holly	Turquoise

This Book Belongs To

My birth date _____

My birth flower _____

My birthstone _____

On my next birthday I will be _____ years old

My Birthday Party

A great party takes lots of hard work. Before you send out your invitations, get some paper, a pencil, and a calendar, and sit down with one of your parents to discuss what you want. You will have to decide on the day, the time, how many guests to invite, where the party will be, and what kind of party you will have.

My birthday party is on this day _____

_____

It will begin at this time _____

It will be over at this time _____

This is where it will be _____

_____

_____

My Party Theme

*If your birthday is in the fall or winter, you could have
a video slumber party or an ice-skating and sledding party.*

*If your birthday is in the spring or summer, you could have
a garden tea party or a cookout party.*

This is the kind of party I will be having _____
_____
_____

Some of the themes I have had for my other birthday
parties are _____
_____
_____
_____
_____
_____
_____
_____
_____
_____
_____

Things We Will Do

*If your birthday is indoors, you can
play telephone, truth-or-dare, or charades.*

*If your birthday is outdoors, you can organize a treasure
hunt, play Marco Polo in the pool, or run relay races.*

These are some of the things we will do _____

_____

_____

_____

_____

_____

_____

_____

_____

_____

_____

_____

_____

_____

Food We Will Eat

If your birthday is in the fall or winter, you can serve hot chocolate and whipped cream, s'mores, or caramel and candied apples.

If your birthday is in the spring or summer, you can serve raspberry and lemon ices, hot fudge sundaes, or chocolate-dipped strawberries.

I will be serving these kinds of food _____

_____

_____

_____

_____

_____

_____

_____

_____

_____

_____

_____

_____

_____

_____

_____

Decorations

If your birthday is in the fall or winter,
you can decorate your party with pumpkins and
autumn leaves, holly, popcorn strings, or paper angels.

If your birthday is in the spring or summer,
you can decorate your party with baskets of flowers,
bows and ribbons, or lots of colored streamers.

My decorations will be_____

_____

_____

_____

_____

_____

_____

_____

Goodie Bags

If your birthday is in the fall or winter, you can give everyone red-and-white peppermint sticks, a pair of pretty socks, or a glass or china animal.

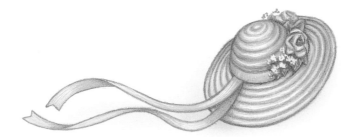

If your birthday is in the spring or summer, you can give everyone tiny violets, miniature tea sets, or straw hats with flowers.

My goodie bags will contain _____

_____

_____

_____

_____

_____

_____

_____

_____

My Birthday Guests

The best parties are the ones with your closest friends and also people you are just beginning to know—like the new girl in school or your neighbor down the street.

These are the people I will invite:

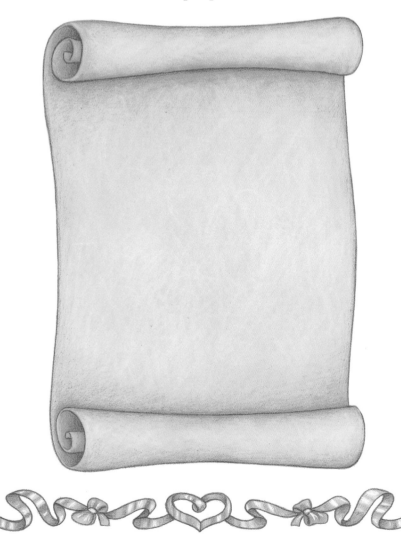

My Invitation

Send out your invitations about two or three weeks before the party, so everyone has enough time to plan to come. And remember, you can make your own invitations—just use some construction paper, glitter, colored pencils, and your imagination!

(PASTE YOUR BIRTHDAY
INVITATION HERE)

"Will you come to my party?" Laura asked
Christy and Maud and Nellie Oleson.
ON THE BANKS OF PLUM CREEK

My Birthday Wishes

These are some of the things I would like for my
birthday _____

_____

_____

_____

_____

_____

_____

_____

_____

_____

_____

_____

_____

_____

_____

_____

_____

_____

_____

My Birthday Day!

When I woke up _____

My first thoughts _____
_____

The weather _____

Events in the news _____
_____

My horoscope _____
_____
_____

These people called to wish me a happy birthday
_____
_____
_____
_____

My Family Birthday

The first thing my mother said _____

_____

The first thing my father said _____

_____

The first things my sisters and brothers said _____

_____

Special things my family did for me on my birthday

_____

_____

My birthday breakfast _____

_____

_____

That night, for a special birthday treat, Pa played
"Pop! Goes the Weasel" for Laura.
LITTLE HOUSE IN THE BIG WOODS

At School or Camp

Depending on when your birthday is, you might have a birthday celebration at school or camp.

What we did _____

_____

What we ate _____

_____

Some things people said to me _____

_____

_____

(PASTE A PHOTOGRAPH OF YOUR

PARTY AT SCHOOL OR CAMP HERE)

My Party Outfit

What I wore _____

_____

_____

_____

Was this a new outfit? _____

_____

(PASTE A PHOTOGRAPH OF YOU

IN YOUR PARTY OUTFIT HERE)

"You look sweet and pretty as posies," Ma said

when they came down the ladder, dressed for the party.

ON THE BANKS OF PLUM CREEK

The Party Begins

Sometimes there can be an awkward silence when
everyone has finally arrived at a party and is wondering what to
do next. One way to make your guests feel more comfortable is to
play a game as soon as everyone has arrived. For example, you
could organize a treasure hunt or play hide-and-seek.

These are the people who came

_____

_____

_____

_____

_____

Who arrived first? _____

Who arrived last? _____

Some things people said when they came in _____

_____

_____

_____

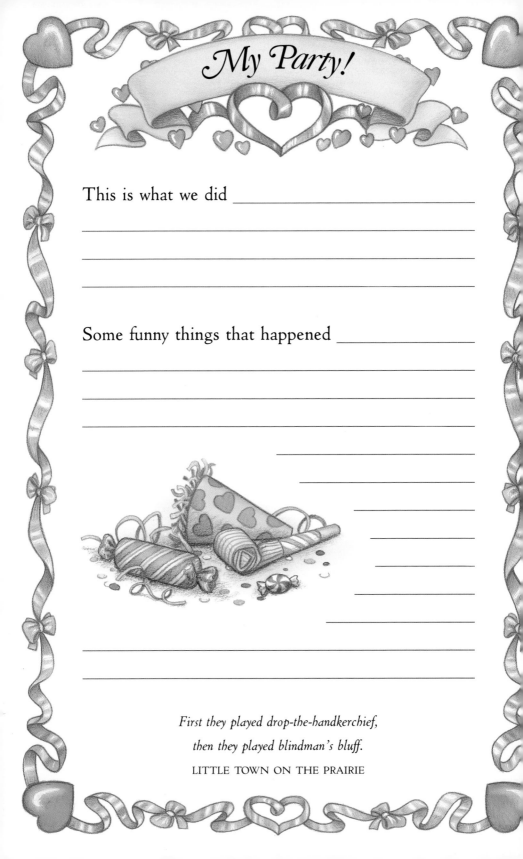

My Party!

This is what we did _____

_____

_____

_____

Some funny things that happened _____

_____

_____

_____

_____

_____

_____

_____

_____

_____

_____

_____

First they played drop-the-handkerchief,

then they played blindman's bluff.

LITTLE TOWN ON THE PRAIRIE

Birthday Autographs

Have all the people who came to your party sign this page

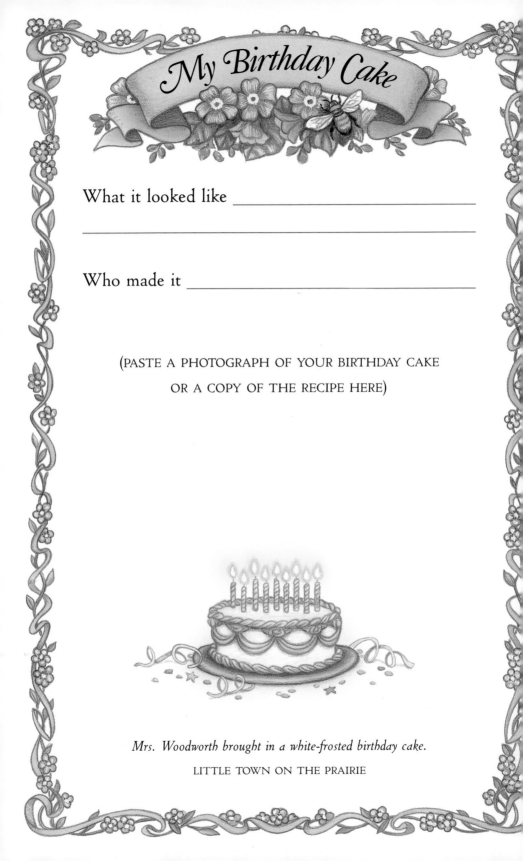

My Birthday Cake

What it looked like _____

_____

Who made it _____

(PASTE A PHOTOGRAPH OF YOUR BIRTHDAY CAKE

OR A COPY OF THE RECIPE HERE)

Mrs. Woodworth brought in a white-frosted birthday cake.

LITTLE TOWN ON THE PRAIRIE

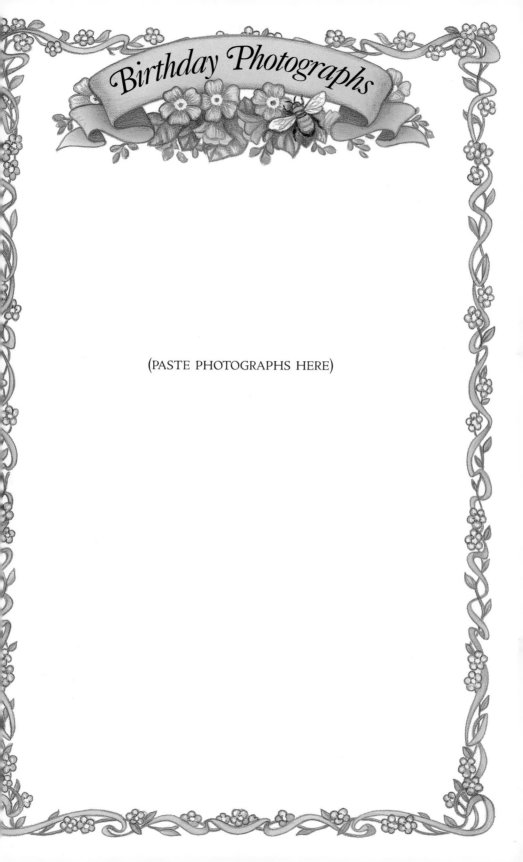

Birthday Photographs

(PASTE PHOTOGRAPHS HERE)

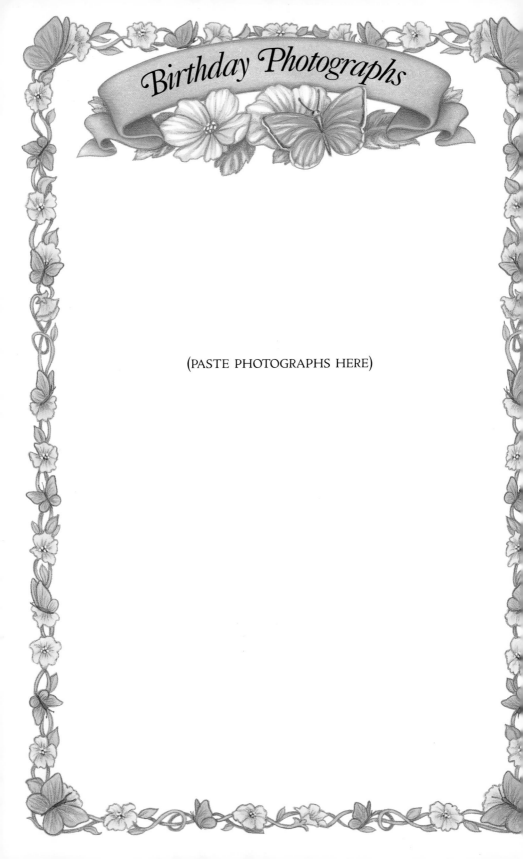

Birthday Photographs

(PASTE PHOTOGRAPHS HERE)

Birthday Photographs

(PASTE PHOTOGRAPHS HERE)

Presents!

These are the presents I received _____

_____

_____

_____

_____

_____

_____

_____

_____

_____

_____

_____

_____

_____

_____

Presents!

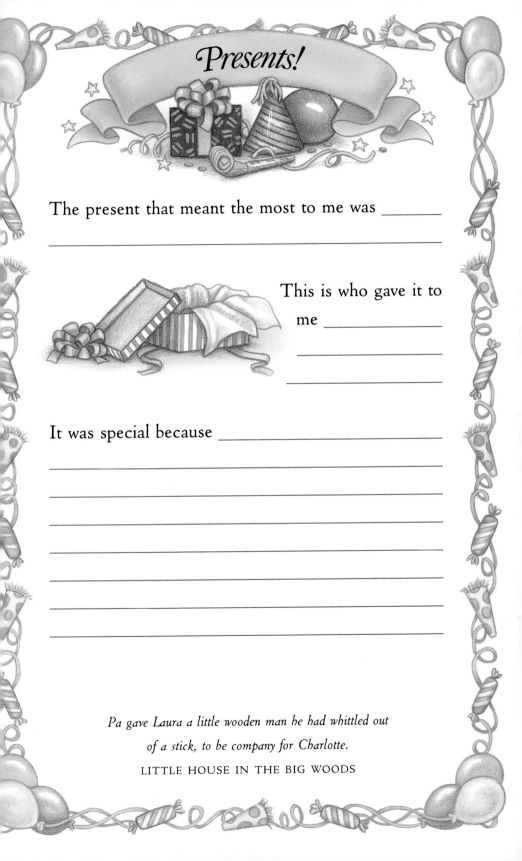

The present that meant the most to me was _____

_____

This is who gave it to

me _____

_____

_____

It was special because _____

_____

_____

_____

_____

_____

_____

_____

_____

Pa gave Laura a little wooden man he had whittled out

of a stick, to be company for Charlotte.

LITTLE HOUSE IN THE BIG WOODS

After the Party

After everyone left, this is what I did _____

_____

_____

This is how I felt _____

_____

_____

_____

_____

_____

_____

_____

_____

_____

Laura only wished the party could have lasted longer.

LITTLE TOWN ON THE PRAIRIE

Birthday Thoughts

The best part of my birthday was _____

_____

_____

_____

_____

_____

_____

_____

_____

_____

_____

The worst part of my birthday was _____

_____

_____

_____

_____

_____

_____

_____

One Year Older

These are some things I would like to accomplish in
the next year _____

_____

_____

_____

_____

_____

_____

_____

_____

_____

_____

_____

_____

_____

_____

_____

_____

_____

_____

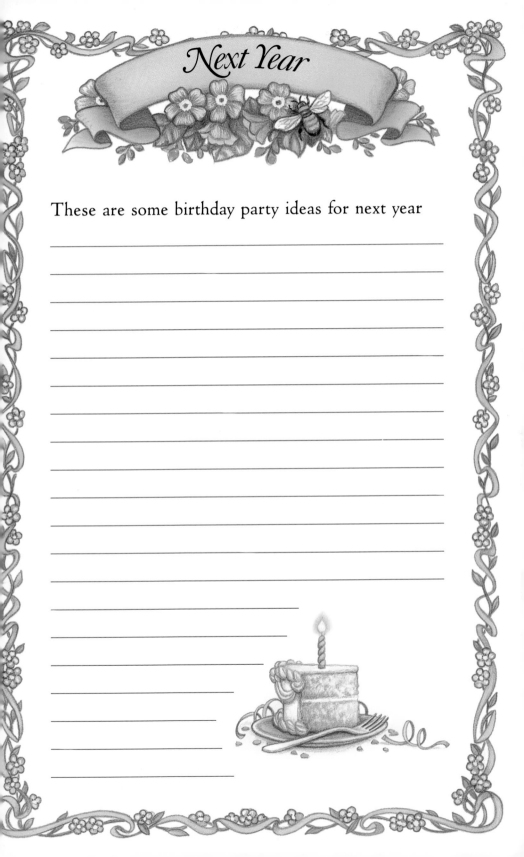

Next Year

These are some birthday party ideas for next year

_____

_____

_____

_____

_____

_____

_____

_____

_____

_____

_____

_____

_____

_____

_____

_____

_____

_____

_____

_____

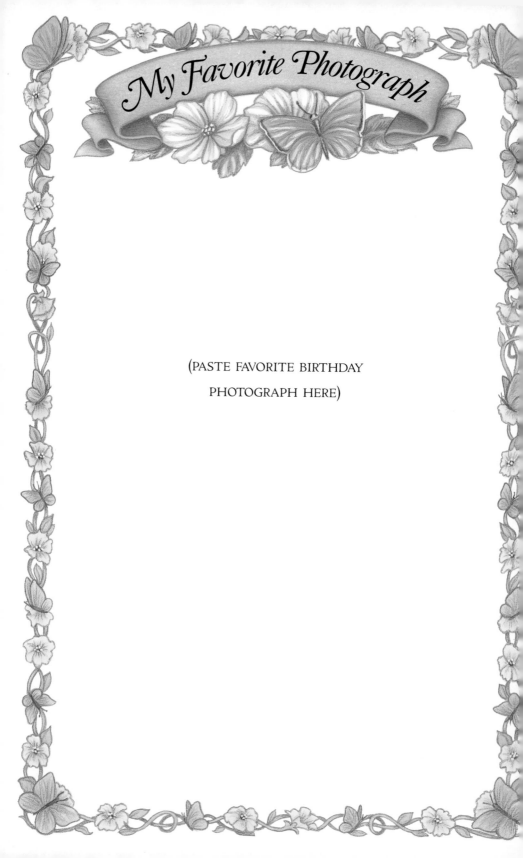

My Favorite Photograph

(PASTE FAVORITE BIRTHDAY

PHOTOGRAPH HERE)